Dear mouse friends,
Welcome to the world of

Geronimo Stilton

THE RODENT'S GAZETTE
EDITORIAL STAFF

Geronimo Stilton
A learned and brainy
mouse; editor of
The Rodent's Gazette

Thea Stilton
Geronimo's sister and
special correspondent at
The Rodent's Gazette

Trap Stilton
An awful joker;
Geronimo's cousin and
owner of the store
Cheap Junk for Less

Benjamin Stilton
A sweet and loving
nine-year-old mouse;
Geronimo's favorite
nephew

Geronimo Stilton

THE WAY OF THE SAMURAI

Scholastic Inc.

New York   Toronto   London   Auckland

Sydney   Mexico City   New Delhi   Hong Kong

ISBN 978-0-545-34101-1

Copyright © 2010 by Edizioni Piemme S.p.A., Via Tiziano 32, 20145 Milan, Italy.

International Rights © Atlantyca S.p.A.

English translation © 2012 by Atlantyca S.p.A.

GERONIMO STILTON names, characters, and related indicia are copyright, trademark, and exclusive license of Atlantyca S.p.A. All rights reserved. The moral right of the author has been asserted.

Based on an original idea by Elisabetta Dami.
www.geronimostilton.com

Published by Scholastic Inc., 557 Broadway, New York, NY 10012. SCHOLASTIC and associated logos are trademarks and/or registered trademarks of Scholastic Inc.

Stilton is the name of a famous English cheese. It is a registered trademark of the Stilton Cheese Makers' Association. For more information, go to www.stiltoncheese.com.

Text by Geronimo Stilton
Original title *Il segreto dei tre samurai*
Cover by Giuseppe Ferrario
Illustrations by Blasco Pisapia and Danilo Barozzi
Color by Romina Denti and Christian Aliprandi
Graphics by Marta Lorini

Special thanks to Kathryn Cristaldi
Translated by Lidia Morson Tramontozzi
Interior design by Kay Petronio

12 11 10 9 8 7 6 5 4 3 2 1   12 13 14 15 16 17/0

Printed in the U.S.A.   40
First printing, April 2012

YOU'RE AS EXCITING AS A RAW CLAM!

Dear rodent **friends**, do you know me? My name is Stilton, *Geronimo Stilton*. I run *The Rodent's Gazette*, the most famouse **newspaper** on Mouse Island. I'm also a bestselling author!

Hello!

I love to write about my amazing **ADVENTURES**. In fact, the one I'm going to tell you about now just might make your **FUR** stand on end! It takes place in a **Mysterious** location. But let me start from the beginning. . . .

It was a typical Saturday Night. I was at home in my cozy mouse hole. I had just finished my typical Saturday Night dinner: one large cheese pizza, one large mozzarella milk shake, and one large cheese Danish. I put on my typical Saturday Night outfit: pj's and cat-fur slippers.

Then I *sank* into my favorite pawchair and began leafing through my photo albums. I love my photo albums! They remind me of all the great trips I've taken.

Yep, it's hard to believe that a **scaredy-mouse** like me has had many incredible

adventures all over the world — but I have! And along the way, I've made many wonderful new friends.

I looked at a photo of me and two **friends**: Wild Willie, an archaeologist, and Shorty Tao, a karate world champion. A while back Shorty asked me (well, okay, she forced me!) to enter a competition in San Mouscisco: the **Karate World Championship**. . . . And I won!

I smiled. What an amazing adventure!

I wrote all about it in my book *The Karate Mouse*. I love to write about my real-life experiences . . . especially when they happen in *exciting* places.

Still, even though I love having adventures, I'm a homebody at heart. That's right: I'm not crazy about traveling! I hate living out of a suitcase and I hate airplanes.

I was thinking about how much I don't like **traveling** when the phone rang.

"Hello? This is Stilton here. *Geronimo Stilton!*" I squeaked.

"Stilton, are you ready for adventure?" said a deep voice.

I gulped. It was my treasure-hunting friend, **Wild Willie**! The last time we were together was in the Black Hills of South Dakota. And let me just tell you: There is a reason they call him **WILD**!

"Um, well, I — I was just relaxing . . . ," I stammered.

Willie snorted. "Relaxing! You were sitting around like a **couch potato**, Stilton. I can just see you in your pajamas and slippers. Did anyone ever tell you *you're as exciting as a raw clam*?" he bellowed.

"Well, I . . . ," I began again.

"'Well, I' nothing!" Willie interrupted. "Now stop **twisting** your tail and listen up. I want you to meet me tonight at eight thirty at **18 South Paw Square**. No ifs, ands, or buts!"

"How d-d-did you know I was t-t-twisting my tail?" I stammered.

But there was no reply. Willie had hung up on me.

What could I do?

I **QUICKLY** got dressed and ran to 18 South Paw Square.

★★★
Wild Willie

★ **WHO HE IS:** An archaeologist who loves adventure. He describes himself as a "treasure hunter," but he actually doesn't care a hoot about the money. In fact, he donates all the archaeological treasures he finds to New Mouse City's mouseum.

★ **HIS MOTTO:** "Are you ready for adventure?" If you answer yes, he'll reply, "Go with the adventure!"

★ **HIS HOBBIES:** Studying ancient languages (such as Egyptian and Mayan) and doing sports (his favorites are karate and mountain climbing).

★ **HIS SECRET:** He keeps a photo of his girlfriend in his shirt pocket, next to his heart.

You're Late!

When I reached South Paw Square, I looked around. What an unusual place. There was an odd-looking **cobblestone** courtyard with a garden filled with strange, exotic-looking plants. In the center of the garden was a **fountain** spouting jets of water onto **round** gray pebbles. The sound of the water hitting the pebbles made me sleepy, and for a minute I thought about taking a quick ratnap. But then I remembered I was supposed to be meeting Wild Willie.

Where was he?

I looked around. I saw lots of buildings facing the courtyard, including a **KARATE dojo**!

Do you know what a karate dojo is? It's a

place where mice practice **KARATE**. I noticed there was a poster on the front door. It said something about a **convention** and . . . what was this??? Why was **MY NAME** listed on the poster?! My stomach lurched as I took a closer look.

THE ZEN DOJO IS HAPPY
TO PRESENT THE LARGEST
CONVENTION ON KARATE
SECRETS EVER! WITH PRACTICAL
DEMONSTRATIONS GIVEN BY OUR
AMAZING GUEST OF HONOR,
WW, AND HIS ASSISTANT,
GERONIMO STILTON.

What is this???

I tried to make out the name of the guest of honor, but I couldn't tell if it was initials (was it W.W.?) or some **strange** symbol.

I took a pawstep closer to see if I could figure it out when suddenly a huge group of rodents appeared behind me. They began *PUSHING* and shoving so they could get into the dojo. **Holey cheese!** I thought. *That convention must be really interesting!*

I recognized a lot of **reporters** and photographers from New Mouse City, including newscasters from the station **TOP TV**!

I was still feeling confused and a little worried when suddenly two paws grabbed me roughly and dragged me into the dojo. . . .

Hee, hee, hee!

Heeeeeeeeeelp!

It was Wild Willie!!!

"How do you like my friends' gym, Stilton?" he squeaked.

Before I could answer, he grabbed me by my whiskers and dragged me down a long hallway. At the end was a stage.

"Go on, Stilton. **YOU'RE LATE!**" he told me, pushing me onto the stage.

I had no idea what Willie was squeaking about. What was I late for? What was going

on? I stood on the stage, feeling like a **fool**, while photographers snapped my picture. I looked for Willie, but he was gone.

I was having trouble seeing with all the **FLASHING** cameras directed at me. At this point the crowd began clapping and shouting.

"There he is! He's coming! That's **HIM**!" they cheered.

I turned **red** with embarrassment. I'm used to fans asking for my autograph. After all, my books are bestsellers. But I'm still a SHY mouse at heart.

"Um, thank you," I mumbled, taking a bow.

Then someone in the audience pointed at me.

"Hey you, **move** over! He's coming!" he shouted.

"Huh? **Who's 'he'?**" I asked, perplexed.

KIAIII!

At that exact moment, I heard a loud yell: "**KIAIII!**"

I barely had time to realize that the yell was that of someone who practices karate and is about to attack when I saw a mass of **MUSCLES** dressed in white hurling himself across the stage. He was so fast it looked as if he was practically *FLYING*.

I tried to move aside, but it was too late.

A paw shot out and kicked me in the tail, sending me *FLYING* into the audience.

"**Heeeeelp!**" I cried.

What a rodent!

I found myself in the arms of a female.

"Youch!" I sobbed, rubbing my tail.

The crowd applauded. It was only then that it dawned on me that they were not cheering for me. They were cheering for the rodent who had taken me out!

He was wearing a white karate uniform with a black belt, and had a black mustache. Do you know who I'm talking about?

Yep, it was Wild Willie!

Let me just say that Wild Willie is a remarkably **ATHLETIC** mouse. Watching him practice karate is like watching a **FLYING DRAGON**.

Wild Willie turned toward the audience and bowed. "Ladies and gentlemice, thank you for coming to this convention dedicated to karate, an ancient **MARTIAL ART** that allows mice to defend themselves without the use of weapons. The object of the sport is to shape the body, **mind**, and spirit.

"The first thing karate teaches is **respect** for oneself and respect for the opponent. And now, before we begin the demonstration, I

would like to thank my fabumouse assistant, *Geronimo Stilton*!"

"Assistant? Who, m-me?" I stammered.

Wild Willie shot me a look and whispered, "Of course! Do you see anyone else on the **STAGE** whose name is Stilton? Now just clam up and go with it."

I shook my head. "But what am I supposed to do? I don't remember much about **KARATE**," I told Willie.

He just smirked. "Don't worry about anything, Stilton. Leave everything up to me!" he ordered.

A minute later Willie came racing toward me. With three very *swift* moves, he FLₐTTEℕED me completely!

The crowd went wild.

"**WOOOOHOOOO!**" they cheered.

Willie picked me up like a bag of cheese

puffs and stood me on my paws.

"You see, in only a few seconds I was able to take out my opponent using just a few basic **KARATE** techniques. As long as you concentrate, you, too, can achieve these results!" he declared.

Then, Willie made sure everyone understood by demonstrating the three kicks again, sending me **crashing** to the floor.

Oh, when would this **NIGHTMARE** end?!

In the meantime, the audience continued to **cheek** and **squeak** with delight.

"Yeah! Good job! Do it **again**!" they cried.

"Ouch! Ouch! Ouch!" I screamed in pain. Couldn't these mice see I was **HURT**? I tried to get Willie's attention, but he was too **pumped up** by the crowd.

"N-n-not ag-g-gain!" I whimpered.

But Willie kept kicking.

Finally, when I was sure every bone in my body had been broken, Willie stopped and bowed to the audience.

"And now, a BANDAGE break for Geronimo while we watch a video on karate," he announced.

While everyone was watching the video, I tried slipping out the back door, but Willie grabbed me by the whiskers.

"This is a **BANDAGE** break, not the end of the show, Stilton! And what's with all the whining? It's an **HONOR** to be my assistant! Do you know how many mice would **kill** to be in your position?" he scolded me.

Would kill for it? I'm being killed! I thought. But out loud I said, "There are **volunteers**? Where are they? I'll gladly switch places!"

Willie shook his head. "Forget it, Stilton," he squeaked. "I'm doing it for your own

Chop Chop

Lotus Snout

good! Just try not to embarrass yourself in front of my friends **CHOP CHOP** and **LOTUS SNOUT**. It's their dojo, after all. And, by the way, your family is here, too."

He pointed to a large rat with **blonde** fur and a **slim** rodent with a black ponytail. Next to them, I saw my entire family!

My eyes nearly popped out of my head. Rats! I couldn't embarrass myself with all of them there! So I let myself be **mangled** by Wild Willie to the very end of the demonstration without complaint.

Finally, he bowed to the audience, everyone applauded, and I slid down the stage with every bone in my body creaking. I had been **trampled** on like a doormat and **beaten** up like a double-cheese milk shake, and **BANDAGED** from the tip of my whiskers to the tip of my tail.

ARE YOU READY FOR ADVENTURE?

While the enthusiastic audience was leaving the dojo, the reporters **SHOUTED**, "Geronimo, tomorrow you'll be on the front page of all the papers!"

The producer of Top TV added, "We're featuring a karate special tonight on our **World News** segment. Our viewers *love* Wild Willie!"

I **cringed**. Just what I needed — my terrified face plastered on every newspaper

and television around the world! How **embaRRassing**! Still, I didn't have time to think about it, because Wild Willie slapped me super **HARD** on the shoulder.

"**Good job**, Stilton! You were the perfect assistant out there," he said.

"Uh, well, thank you. I did my **best**, or maybe my **worst**. What I mean is, I did whatever I could . . . ," I babbled.

I noticed Chop Chop and Lotus Snout staring at me intently.

"I think he's **perfect**, Willie," Chop Chop said.

"Yes, just the mouse for the job," Lotus Snout agreed.

I had no idea what they were talking about. **What job?**

Wild Willie grinned. Then he thumped me on the back, making my teeth **rattle**.

"Stilton, we've decided you need to get out more," he **announced**.

"What do you mean?" I squeaked, a feeling of _**dread**_ coming over me.

It was then that I noticed the rest of my family staring at me.

Thea chimed in. "We think you're becoming a **couch potato**. When was the last time you took a trip?"

"Ahem, well, it's been a while," I admitted. "But I have **so much** to do at work and you know that I hate traveling —"

Willie interrupted me. "Oh, don't be such a travel baby, Stilton! Now are you ready for adventure? **Yes or No?**" he shouted.

I gulped. I wanted to say no. I mean, Willie's idea of adventure is my idea of torture. But everyone was staring at me. What could I do? "I guess so . . . ," I muttered.

"Great! Go with the **adventure**! We're headed for Japan!'" roared Wild Willie.

Trap handed me a teensy-weensy **SUITCASE**.

"We know you're a pack rat, so we packed for you. This suitcase has all you need: your **KARATE** uniform, a **toothbrush**, and a tourist **GUIDE**."

Grandfather William added, "Make me proud, Grandson. **OR ELSE!**"

Wild Willie chuckled.

"Isn't this great, Stilton? Now you'll have something to write about when you get back. That is, if you make it back **alive**," he said with a smirk.

I tried not to think about the other possibility as Benjamin planted a *kiss* on my snout.

"Have a good time, Uncle Geronimo!" he squeaked.

One hour later I boarded a **plane** with Wild Willie, Chop Chop, and Lotus Snout. We were on a **long** flight to Tokyo, the capital of Japan, and then planned to head south to the island of **Okinawa**, where karate is said to have been born.

During the flight, I flipped through the guide to Japan.

WHAT A FASCINATING COUNTRY . .

JAPAN

Japan is an island lying off the east coast of Asia in the Pacific Ocean. It is made up of four main islands (Honshu, Hokkaido, Kyushu, and Shikoku) and numerous smaller islands. Japan is known as the Land of the Rising Sun, because it lies to the east of China. The capital of Japan is Tokyo.

SHREWDPAWS KNOWS EVERYTHING

At the airport in Tokyo, a **CHAUFFEUR** dressed in dark clothes greeted us.

"Wild Willie-san?" he asked as he bowed deeply. "Mr. Shrewdpaws invited you to his house. He wants to talk with you."

Wild Willie twirled his **mustache** and slowly blinked.

"Hmmm . . . Shrewdpaws. I haven't heard that name in many years. How did he know we were **coming**?" he asked, surprised.

The driver bowed, stone-faced.

"Shrewdpaws knows everything," he said.

"Well then, take us to him," grumbled Wild Willie.

Wild Willie-san *means "Mr. Wild Willie."*

The chauffeur bowed and said, "Please follow me."

Then he led us to his car — the most luxurious limousine I had ever seen. It was **extremely long**, with a shiny black exterior and TINTED glass. We arrived in Tokyo at dawn. It was breathtaking! Thousands of SKYSCRAPERS shimmered majestically under the first rays of the sun.

The limo zoomed along the crowded streets, where FRENZIED cars circled the center of the city. I admired the marvelous ancient buildings and the splendid gardens in the old section of Tokyo.

What a magnificent city!

I took one PICTURE after another. Here are some of them. ⋯⋯⋯⋯⋯

While the chauffeur drove, Wild Willie pulled us all together.

Ginza: Known for the most fabumouse shopping, this district has huge department stores, designer boutiques, and many wonderful restaurants.

Tokyo's skyscrapers

Akihabara: This area is known for having the most stores that sell electronic equipment, such as high-tech computers, cell phones, and video games.

A typical garden in Tokyo

Kabuki Theater: Opened in 1889 but closed in 2010, it was known for serious Japanese entertainment, including music and dance performances.

"I want to tell you all the real reason for this trip to Japan. We are about to have an adventure that may become **VEEEEEEEEEEERY DANGEROUS** . . . ," he whispered.

I shivered.

"The **teacher** who taught me karate many years ago asked me to help him save an ancient treasure: an important *parchment*," Wild Willie explained.

This piqued Lotus Snout's interest.

"Why is it so important?" she asked.

"Because it holds an **ancient KARATE secret**. And someone is out to steal it,"

Geronimo Stilton

answered Wild Willie with a frown.

"Who?" asked Lotus Snout.

Wild Willie stroked his mustache. "I don't know, but I bet we'll soon find out. Maybe it's **SHREWDPAWS**," he mumbled.

I was horrified.

"B-b-but then why did we agree to go to his h-h-house?" I squeaked, feeling a **PANIC ATTACK** coming on.

Willie just smiled. "We need to find out what he wants. Maybe he can give us a **clue** to help our mission," he said. "Look at it this way, Stilton — now you'll have something to write about when you get home. That is, if you make it back **alive**."

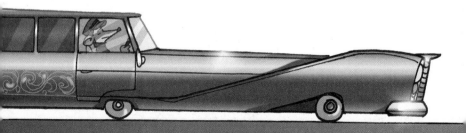

WATCH OUT FOR THE WASABI, GERONIMO!

Before I could jump out of the limo and run away SQUEAKING with fear, we rolled up to an elegant house built in the traditional Japanese style. It was made of wood, with a large roof decorated with four dragons. Surrounding the house was a magnificent garden complete with GURGLING fountains, incredible rock formations, and many bonsai trees.

A large flashy rodent with shifty eyes and a black toupee on his head came to greet us.

"My name is *Spencer Shrewdpaws*. Welcome to my fabumouse home," he announced arrogantly.

Bonsai *are dwarf trees.*

Welcome!

Then he began to brag about himself.

"As you can see by my house, I am a very **RiCH** — and therefore a very important — mouse here in Japan. You should also know I am a **grand master** of karate, and I was a student of the famous *Noblemouse*," he said.

Wild Willie raised an eyebrow.

"I, too, have become a **grand master** of karate, and I, too, was a student of **Noblemouse**. But maybe you have forgotten his teachings. Being **RiCH** does not make you important," he declared.

Shrewdpaws turned **red** with anger, but he stroked his toupee and motioned for us to follow him. Wild Willie removed his boots (in Japanese homes, one enters **without shoes**), and I followed. As I looked around me, I had the strange feeling

Look....

This is how ...

they are held!

And you eat!

that someone was watching us. From the window I thought I saw **MYSTERIOUS DARK SHADOWS**.

I was still thinking about those **shadows** when Shrewdpaws's voice interrupted my thoughts.

"And now you will eat. My chef has prepared a sampling of the most exquisite Japanese dishes, complete with lots of wasabi," he declared.

Wild Willie winked at me.

"*Watch out for the wasabi, Stilton,*" he warned.

Wasabi? What was that? But there was no time to ask. Before I knew it, we were

seated at a low **TABLE** covered with lots of small dishes filled with food.

Chop Chop tried to show me how to use the chopsticks.

But it was no use. I tried hard to imitate him, but the chopsticks kept slipping from my paws. First I stuck one of the sticks into my **eye**. Then the other got stuck in my **ear**. And then both sticks got stuck up my **nose**!

Meanwhile, Shrewdpaws's waiter kept bringing us more bowls filled with strange food: rice rolls, little morsels of raw fish, rolls wrapped in seaweed, and a strange green paste.

"*Watch out for the wasabi, Stilton,*"
Wild Willie warned me again.

Wasabi? What was that? I still had no idea!

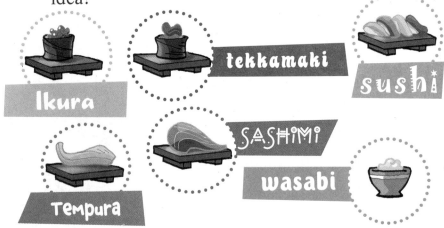

I tried my best to keep an open mind about eating all the **DiFFeRent** foods. After all, my great-aunt Ratilda always told me, "Variety is the **spice** of life when it comes to meals." But I have to admit, nothing seemed to have much flavor. Oh, what I would have given for a large **CHEESE PiZZA**!

Ikura, tekkamaki, sushi, sashimi, *and* tempura are typical Japanese dishes.

My stomach grumbled as I dreamed of **The Slice Rat**. Have you ever been there? They make the best pizza on all of Mouse Island. I had a feeling there was no Slice Rat in the area, though, so instead I took a nibble of fish.

Then I made a big mistake. I spread a piece of fish with a lump of the **strange** green paste.

Wild Willie tried to stop me.

"Watch out for the wasabi, Stilton!" he shouted.

Too late! I had already swallowed it.

I soon found out that wasabi was the name of that strange green paste. It was so spicy, tears ran down my fur and flames

Watch out for the wasabi!

Wasabi *is a very spicy Japanese paste made from the greenish root of an Asian herb. It is similar in flavor to horseradish.*

shot out of my mouth, setting Shrewdpaws's toupee on **FIRE**.

Without blinking an eye, Wild Willie poured tea on Shrewdpaws's head to put out the fire. **Oh, how humiliating!**

I Am a Rich and Powerful Mouse!

I tried apologizing to Shrewdpaws, but he was LIVID. "What is the matter with you, Cheesebrain!" he shrieked. He stomped out of the room and returned wearing a new toupee.

"Now listen up, Wild Willie-san. I don't know much about your cheesebrain friend here, but I know many things about you. I know you are a famous treasure hunter on Mouse Island and an expert in KARATE. I also know you spent many years in Japan. That is why I have decided you must help me.

"Recently, the ruins of the **Castle of the**

Roaring Dragon were found in the Roaring Dragon Valley.

"According to an **ancient legend**, a parchment of incredible value is hidden in that castle," Shrewdpaws continued. "It is said to give great *power* to the one possessing it. I want you to explore the castle and find me that parchment. **I MUST HAVE IT!** Just name your price."

Wild Willie rolled his eyes.

"You seem to know a lot about me, Shrewdpaws, but you forgot one important detail: **I am not for sale**!"

Shrewdpaws whipped out his checkbook and DIAMOND-STUDDED gold pen. "Oh, don't be ridiculous, Willie, every mouse can be bought! Just write down a figure!" he insisted.

Wild Willie **stood** up. "Forget it,

Shrewdpaws!" he said. "I said **NO**! I am an archaeologist with a passion for ancient civilizations. Even if I did find the parchment, I wouldn't give it to you. I'd give it to a **mouseum**. I don't look for treasures to make money. I look for treasures so that everyone can **enjoy** them and **learn** something about the past."

Shrewdpaws was so angry he looked like he was about to **EXPLODE**.

"I am warning you, Willie, I am a very rich and powerful mouse! If you don't help me, I promise you will be one **sorry rodent**!" he shrieked.

Write down a figure!

I said no!

I thought I would faint from **FRIGHT**, but Wild Willie stood his ground.

"I told you, I'm not for sale!" he replied.

We left in a taxi. As we were driving away, I spotted the **MYSTERIOUS SHADOWS** again behind the house.

Still, there was no time to worry about them. We had to run to the station and take the **TRAIN** to Nagoya*, where a ferry would then take us to Okinawa, our original destination.

We boarded the train just in time. I stared out the window and spotted the **DARK, MYSTERIOUS SHADOWS** again. They were the same ones I had seen at Shrewdpaws's house. As I peered more closely, I realized the shadows were actually seven muscular rodents wearing **BLACK CLOTHING** and masks. Their eyes shined dangerously.

48

* See map on page 29.

As the train began to leave the station, I spotted a little mouselet on the platform waving good-bye to the train.

"**Bye-bye!**" I called, waving my paw at the little mouse.

Chop Chop quickly pulled me away from the window.

"**WHAT ARE YOU DOING?!** Why are you waving at those **NINJA**?! They're Japanese warriors. They're experts in the ancient martial arts and very dangerous!" he squeaked.

"But I wasn't waving at them," I said, trying to explain.

Lotus Snout shook her head.

"Your waving **angered** them," she moaned.

Wild Willie just stared out the window with a funny smile on his face.

"Hey, look! The ninja are _running_ after us," he observed calmly. "I wonder if they'll get on the train. That would make it a pretty interesting trip, especially for you, Stilton."

My teeth rattled from fright.

"I-I want to g-get off. I want to t-take the first plane back to N-New Mouse City!" I cried.

Bye-bye!
Bye-bye!
Bye-bye!

I ran down the narrow aisle, but the train was going at a *CRAZY SPEED*! Chop Chop grabbed me by the tail.

"Are you nuts, Stilton? You can't get off! This train is called *Shinkansen,* also known as a bullet train. It travels as fast as 186 miles an hour!"

I went back to my seat, feeling terrified, as trees, houses, and mountains *shot* by at warp speed. My head began to **pound**. I needed to relax. I tried reading my tourist guide about Japan.

HELP!
HELP!
HELP!

Too bad I opened to the section about **NINJA**. Talk about scary!

Ninja were **WARRIORS** *and spies at the service of Japanese military commanders, or shoguns. The ninja code valued completing a mission by whatever means necessary—which included sneak attacks and* **POISONING***.*

They wore black clothing as **dark as night** *and were expert at all martial arts. They used more than twenty types*

Geronimo Stilton →

of killer **WEAPONS**, including swords, daggers, arrows, poisoned arrow tips, javelins, and pikes.

As I was reading, **cold shivers** ran down my fur. I thought I could see strange figures in the train's compartments. Had the ninja boarded the train?

CHEESE NIBLETS! I WAS A WRECK!!!!

I Am Red Dragon

Finally, the high-speed train stopped at Nagoya, and from there we boarded a ferry for Naha*, the capital of Okinawa. **IT WAS A NEVER-ENDING TRIP!** At Naha we got on a bus that took us to a place in the middle of nowhere. The **SUN** was setting behind the mountains as we continued on foot to a little village located between the mountains.

It had been a long time since Wild Willie had visited this place, and he couldn't remember the exact **ROAD** leading to the house of his teacher, **Noblemouse**. After lots of wrong turns, we finally arrived at an ancient **WOODEN** house built on the top of a steep cliff. There was someone sitting in front of the house, but by now it was getting

* See map on page 29.

DARK so it was hard to see his or her face.

As we approached, the rodent called out, "May I help you?"

"We are looking for the honorable karate teacher, Noblemouse, who lives in this village," Wild Willie said.

"Why?" the rodent asked.

Without thinking, I blurted out, "We're here on a secret **mission**!"

Chop Chop stopped me with a jabbing elbow to my side.

Lotus Snout kicked

I found it!

me in the tail, and Wild Willie **PULLED** one of my whiskers.

The shadow moved. I trembled with fear. Then I realized it was just an **old** rodent wearing a very gentle smile and a white karate uniform.

He **laughed**.

"Don't be mad at your friend. He sensed he could trust me. I am the teacher Noblemouse. Who are you?" the rodent asked.

Wild Willie bowed until he touched the ground with his whiskers.

WILD WILLIE AS A YOUNG MOUSE

Teacher...

"Teacher, many years have gone by, but my heart has stayed the same. I promised you could always count on me, and now here I am to keep my promise. I am **RED DRAGON**."

He rolled up his sleeve, revealing a fierce-looking **RED DRAGON** tattoo.

The old rodent's smile widened and a tear glistened in the corner of one eye.

"**RED DRAGON**, is it really you?" he murmured.

Wild Willie knelt before him.

"Yes, teacher, it is I, although now they call me **Wild Willie**. You sent for me, so I have come."

Noblemouse beamed.

"I knew I could count on you, **RED DRAGON**," he said.

"You were always such a good student.

You were courageous and filled with **FIRE**, like a dragon with a strong and generous heart."

Wild Willie and Noblemouse hugged each other affectionately. Then Noblemouse invited us into his house.

"Now we will have a *tea ceremony* to help restore your energy," he declared.

I was so excited I let out a happy **squeak**. A cup of tea sounded great right then. And maybe a sandwich. I was starving!

Lotus Snout shot me a menacing look.

"The tea ceremony is a SPIRITUAL RITUAL. You don't stuff your face!" she warned.

Noblemouse led us to a small, clean, and quiet room. On a table I spotted a striking arrangement of flowers, arranged by the **IKEBANA**

Ikebana *is the ancient Japanese art of cut-flower arrangements.*

method. On a wall I saw a collection of **katana** — samurai swords.

Following Noblemouse's example, we all knelt around a small, low table. Then the elder mouse poured each of us a cup of **green tea**.

I took a sip of my tea, trying not to think about my aching knees. The floor was so hard, my knees were already killing me! I couldn't wait to get up and *stretch* my paws, but just then Noblemouse announced, "I will now tell you the Legend of the Three Samurai, so that you will understand why it is so important to save the parchment."

Many centuries ago . . .

The moon was already shining in the dark sky as the old teacher began the story.

A katana *is a long, single-edged, curved Japanese sword used by samurai.*

Many centuries ago, in a secret and faraway place, there was a mysterious and valuable parchment that held the incredible secret of karate. It was so powerful it could make the strong weak and the weak strong. One day, however, the evil Head of the Ninja tried to steal it. So a wise karate teacher asked three valiant samurai to hide it in a safe place. Those three courageous samurai took the parchment to a faraway valley. There they found the Castle of the Roaring Dragon, which belonged to a wise shogun named Hanshi. The samurai hid the parchment in a secret place in the castle so that no one would ever find it. According to the legend, the parchment must remain hidden in the castle until three other valiant samurai find it. Only then can its secret be revealed to everyone.

A shogun *is a powerful Japanese feudal lord.*

The teacher sighed.

"For a long time the Castle of the Roaring Dragon was just a **legend**. But now its ruins have been found in the valley bearing its name, and I'm afraid that many evil rodents will try to find the *parchment* and abuse its immense power. That is why I called you, Red Dragon — I mean, Wild Willie. I need you to help me save this TREASURE!"

Wild Willie nodded.

"Of course I will help you. I'll do anything to save an ancient TREASURE!" he squeaked.

Everyone smiled except for me. I couldn't. My face was frozen in an expression of pain. It felt like someone was sticking knives into my knees! I had to get up! But to my horror, Noblemouse said, "Now that the tea has restored us in body and spirit, we will stay here **ALL NIGHT** and decide how we will save the parchment."

Stay here all night??!!!

No! I screamed silently. My knees couldn't take another minute! "Ahem, I just need to stand up for a second," I said, excusing myself from the table.

I tried to get up, but my knees wouldn't straighten. I tripped over my own paws and grabbed the display case filled with swords. The swords *TUMBLED* out of the case, cutting off my whiskers in a clean sweep. I crashed into the ikebana and a thorn got stuck in my fur. As I was trying to remove it, I knocked over the kettle and BURNED my tail with boiling tea. *HOPPING* away, I smacked my head against a gong until I saw *stars.* Holey cheese! I sobbed for a moment. Then I fainted.

Three Samurai (and an Ordinary Mouse)

When I came to, I was completely confused. Instead of my regular clothes, I was wearing a floral Japanese tunic. I looked just like an **ancient Japanese** rodent!

I massaged my head. What a lump!

I was thinking about getting an ice pack when I turned and saw three samurai

What's going on?

warriors in complete armor staring at me.

"Help! I want to live!" I shrieked.

The first samurai rolled his eyes.

"Cut the drama, Stilton," he scolded. "The ninja are out to steal this *secret parchment*. It's up to us to save it!"

I realized the samurai was Wild Willie. "Huh?" I mumbled. "Why are you dressed like that?"

The second samurai snickered.

It's up to us!

"Because this is a **dream**, Stilton, and in the dream we are **samurai**."

It was Chop Chop.

"Oh, a dream? How nice! Can I can be a **samurai**, too?" I squeaked.

The third samurai was slim and graceful. It was Lotus Snout.

"Sorry, Stilton. Even in your dreams you'll always be just an **ordinary mouse**." She giggled.

"Rats," I **murmured**.

Wild Willie could tell I was disappointed.

"I'll tell you what, Stilton. I'll keep my eye on you. If you work hard, maybe at the end of this **dream** you can become a real samurai," he suggested.

Then he mounted the saddle of a black horse and shouted, "Let's move! The ninja are after us. We've got to hide this parchment

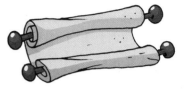

in a safe place."

I gulped. I wasn't much of a horseback rider. Plus I was **afraid of the dark**! But what could I do? I knew Wild Willie was keeping an eye on me. So I climbed onto a horse and followed my friends.

We traveled under a **full moon**, changing directions many times so the ninja would have trouble following us.

Maybe it was my imagination, but I felt like I saw the ninja shadows everywhere we rode.

Cheese niblets! It's tough being a **SCAREDY-MOUSE**!

Finally, we came to a lonely valley lost among the mountains, where a **Waterfall** tumbled down from a rock shaped like the head of a dragon.

"We'll go under the waterfall. It's a secret passageway that will take us to the **ROARING DRAGON VALLEY**," Wild Willie said.

I shivered. The waterfall **TUMBLING** down from the top of the rock sounded exactly like the roar of a dragon. Slimy Swiss rolls! I was so scared I thought I might **faint**! But I had to go on. Wild Willie was watching me. I took a deep breath and rode under the falls. On the other side we came to a lush green valley. A **castle** rose in the distance.

"That castle will be a safe place for the parchment. It belongs to a wise shogun. His name is **Hanshi**, which means 'teacher of the trades,'" Wild Willie explained.

Soon we reached the castle and everyone

slid off their horses and went inside. I, on the other paw, fell off my horse, tripped over my tail, and **STUMBLED** after them. Once inside, I found myself in a room decorated with colorful silk drapes. At one end of the room, there was a stage. In the center of it sat a regal-looking rodent wearing a **red** tunic with a dragon embroidered on it.

The rodent stared at us with deep, penetrating eyes. It was then that I noticed the two massive **GOLD** dragon heads in front of his chair and two more on the armrests. I guess that rodent liked his dragons!

Two rows of fully armed guards stood **WATCHING** our every move.

I tried not to look as **SCARED**

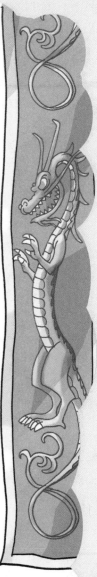

as I felt, but I couldn't stop my whiskers from trembling with fear.

Meanwhile, Wild Willie bowed before the shogun in greeting.

He took out the rolled *parchment* and bowed his head again.

"Honorable shogun **Hanshi**, master of masters, we are here to ask for your help," he said.

"How can I help?" asked the shogun.

"We are being followed by the Head of the Ninja, who wants this *parchment* containing an ancient karate secret. May we **hide** it in your castle?"

The shogun Hanshi thought for a moment and then bowed his head and said, "**Let it be so!**"

He waved his paw and the guards left the room. Then he rested his arms on the throne's GOLDEN armrests and pressed down heavily on them.  We heard a creaking and suddenly the walls before us opened up, revealing a secret room! The shogun produced **seven keys**. Then he opened  **seven chests** nestled neatly one inside the other.

"I will hide the parchment here, in these chests in this **secret** room. No one will ever find it. Its secret will be preserved for hundreds of years, until it is time for it to be revealed," the shogun said.

Then he turned to us.

"You have been very courageous. One can see you are real **samurai**," he remarked.

I turned red.

"Ahem, well, actually, I'm not a real samurai. I'm just **an ordinary mouse**," I confessed.

The shogun looked deeply into my eyes and murmured, "I can fix that."

Then he asked in a loud voice, "Who will vouch for the **COURAGE** of this mouse?"

Wild Willie took a step forward.

"I will vouch for him," he said. "Even though he's basically a scaredy-mouse, on this journey he faced his fears to help protect the parchment. He has the **heart** of a real samurai."

The shogun stared at me.

"Do you promise to keep your spirit

strong and to always follow the way of the **samurai**?" he asked.

"Y-y-yes!" I stammered.

Then the shogun stood up and announced, "You are now a **samurai**!"

You are now a samurai!

I was so honored I bowed deeply to thank him but ended up **tripping** over my tail and **smashing** my head on the floor.

Argh!!

BULL'S-EYE!

I came to because **somebody** was slapping my face as if it were a punching bag at **The Ironpaw Gym** in New Mouse City.

"Wake up, Stilton!" a voice instructed.

It was hard for me to get up. I was out of it. My head was *spinning* and my whiskers were trembling. What was going on? Was I awake or was I dreaming???

Confused, I asked, "W-where am I? Why are you slapping me? Am I still a real samurai?"

I looked around me, and my eyes opened wide.

I was no longer in the Castle of the Roaring Dragon. I was back at karate

master Noblemouse's house. The teakettle was upside down on the floor, the antique swords were scattered next to it, and there was a huge dent in the gong.

Chop Chop, Lotus Snout, and Wild Willie stood looking down at me. They were no longer dressed in their samurai outfits. Instead of a sword, Lotus Snout clutched a **cell phone**.

"He's awake. Should I still call the ambulance?" she asked the others as they examined the watermelon-sized lump on my head. Wild Willie **laughed** silently under his whiskers.

"I think he'll be fine, right, Stilton? That was a great show, though. My favorite part was when you **SLAMMED** the gong with your furry skull. **Bull's-eye!**" He chuckled. "Who knew you had such a hard head!"

Just then it all came back to me: the tea ceremony, my **ACHING** knees, trying to stand up, knocking over the teakettle, and **Slamming** my head into the gong. **Youch!**

I was trying to ignore the ringing in my ears when Wild Willie's voice broke into my thoughts.

"Okay, enough entertaining. Let's shake a paw before the **NINJA** catch up to us. We're off to the Roaring Dragon Valley. We need to find the parchment. It's hidden somewhere inside the castle there," he said.

At that I instantly forgot about my aching head.

"I know exactly where the parchment is. I saw it in my dream!" I squeaked. "It's in a special room in the castle!"

I know where it is!

Chop Chop and Lotus Snout laughed.

"It was only a **dream**, Geronimo. It wasn't real," they said.

But Wild Willie looked me directly in the **EYES**.

"Hmm . . . it does sound strange, but I want to trust you, Stilton," he said.

"I **promise** you won't be sorry!" I squeaked. "Everyone follow me!"

It was 𝔻𝔸𝕎ℕ as we took off down the road. Noblemouse stayed behind to alert all the farmers in his village to the ninja who were coming. He promised to

The castle as it was in the dream

join us as soon as he had gathered everyone.

By the first rays of the morning's sun, we arrived in the lonely valley. I recognized the waterfall tumbling down from a rock shaped like the head of a dragon. I went under the falls and I headed straight through the **SECRET** passageway.

At the other side of the falls were the **Roaring Dragon Valley** and, beyond that, Hanshi's castle. Everything was just like in the dream, but the castle was in ruins, as if **hundreds and hundreds** of years had gone by.

The castle as it is today

THE LEGEND OF THE
THREE SAMURAI

The roof of the castle was **crumbling** and the red paint had all but peeled away. Large overgrown bamboo shrubs swayed forlornly in the wind, and the stairs were cracked and caked with dirt.

We began to walk toward the castle. Our steps **ECHOED** on the big gray stones in the path. My heart was **POUNDING** a mile a minute. Did I mention that I hate **SPOOKY** stuff?

Just then Wild Willie murmured, "Are you ready for adventure?"

"**Yes!**" the others answered immediately.

As for me, I was too busy biting my

nails. Oh, how I wished I were home in my comfy, cozy mouse hole!

We entered the castle, but before we **CLOSED** the front door behind us, we checked to see if the ninja were following us. Luckily, there were no ninja in sight.

It was as dark as **NIGHT** in the castle, and the air was thick and **musty**. I lit a candle with shaky paws.

I tried to concentrate on not **BURNING** myself.

I looked around. **Dust** covered every object in the room, and **cobwebs** hung from the ceiling. Still, the room looked the same as I remembered it from my dream.

Even if time had destroyed much of it, I recognized the stage with the **red** chair the shogun had sat in. And the armrests were shaped like the heads of **DRAGONS**,

just like in my dream.

If everything was like the **dream**, then the parchment had to be here!

"In my dream, the shogun pushed the armrests of the chair and a SECRET room appeared," I mumbled.

Then I sat slowly down on the chair. My whiskers **trembled**. I was so nervous! I pushed hard on the two armrests. Nothing happened. My heart sank to my paws. But then I heard a tiny **creak**.

Then another **creak**! And another **creeeeeeeeeeeeeaaaaaaaak**!!!!

On the wooden wall before us, a tiny crevice appeared. I squeezed myself through. **"Follow me!"** I shouted.

On the other side of the crevice was a small room, which I remembered well. Light had not penetrated that room until now, so the **colors** were not faded, and it seemed that time had stood still. In a corner was an antique lacquered wooden chest and a ring of keys. The chest was identical to the one in my dream! I opened it with a key and took out another chest, then another, and another,

It should be here!

then another and another. Finally, I got to the last PRIZED chest.

I took out the *parchment*, which was tied with a red *silk ribbon*. When I saw it, I was speechless.

It was identical to the one I had seen in my dream!

HERE'S THE LEGENDARY PARCHMENT!

The only difference was that it was yellowed and fragile, as if years — even centuries — had gone by since my dream.

I was so *excited* I could hardly squeak! I could hardly believe my dream had turned out to be reality! And now that we had found the parchment, we could finally discover its SECRET!

TELL ME
WHAT IT SAYS!

Wild Willie took the parchment, read it, and **muttered**, "Hmmm . . . interesting, very interesting."

"So, what's the secret in the parchment?" I asked.

He looked at me, then back at the parchment.

"Hmmmm . . . **interesting**, very interesting," he said again.

I twisted my tail in a knot. "Okay, we get that it's **interesting**, but what does it say?" I insisted.

Willie blinked.

"Actually, it's a lot more **interesting**

than you might think," he continued.

I bit my tongue to stop myself from **screaming**. But it was no use. I couldn't take it anymore. "Tell me!" I shrieked. "Tell me what it says!"

Wild Willie twirled his mustache and stared at me.

"Really, Stilton. You need to learn how to have **P-A-T-I-E-N-C-E**. Do you know the

meaning of the word?" he said with a smirk.

I tried to calm down but I was feeling so impatient I thought I might **EXPLODE** in a cloud of fur!

Finally, Willie held out the parchment. Unfortunately, I couldn't read a thing. There was a lot of **Japanese** writing and a drawing showing a figure with red **Dots** on it.

"This parchment explains all about pressure points. It is said that the body has certain areas that correspond to **centers of energy**. Touching them at specific points can **Heal** or **immobilize** a rodent," Willie said. "This ancient technique was used by samurai long ago."

He studied the parchment intensely. "Let's see if it works. Come here, Stilton," he commanded.

I blinked. "Do we really have to try it?" I whined.

"Of course!" Willie said, shaking his head. "Don't be such a scaredy-mouse!"

Thrilled, Chop Chop and Lotus Snout shouted, "Yes, come on, yes, yes, yes, yes. Let's try it!"

Before I knew it, Wild Willie lightly brushed his paw against my chin. Within seconds, I **CRASHED** to the floor like a brick of stale cheese. *SNAP!*

Everybody cheered.

"It works!"

I sat up and rubbed my **ACHING** tail. "Why do I always have to be the assistant?" I mumbled. But of course, no one was listening.

Wild Willie had begun translating the rest of the parchment.

"It says here this ancient and mysterious technique is called *TUITE*," he said. "It allows the weak to overcome the strong and gives the unarmed a chance to defend themselves when attacked. It's not based on force, but on **AGILITY**, *SWIFTNESS*, and **KNOWLEDGE** of the pressure points.

TUITE

Tuite is a traditional karate fighting technique. It is based on attacking certain pressure points on the body by grabbing the opponent. Pressure points must be hit at the correct angle. It is used in self-defense.

It's to be used only in self-defense, and never to attack someone."

At this, Wild Willie nodded. "That's so true. My karate teacher always said, 'The wise mouse values **peace**, not conflict.'"

Willie had us memorize all the pressure points.

There were **tons** of them all over the body! Who knew?

Is there one here?

Yep, on your elbow!

Very cool!

STICK UP YOUR PAWS!

We were still checking out the pressure points when a voice cried out, "STICK UP YOUR PAWS!"

We turned to see a rodent with evil eyes.

It was Shrewdpaws!!!

He was followed by seven rodents dressed in black and armed to the teeth. The **NINJA!**

I felt faint with fear. How could we defend ourselves? There were **eight** of them and only **four** of us! Plus they were armed!

Headlines *flashed* across my brain: *Stilton Sliced by Ninja Swords! Puny*

Publisher Pummeled in Japan!

But just then Willie whispered, "Remember the **SECRET** of the parchment!"

We began defending ourselves using the technique we had learned.

One by one the ninja fell to the ground like **lumpy** old cheese rinds. A few minutes later, Master Noblemouse and all the farmers in his village showed up to help.

But thanks to the secret of the parchment, the weak had conquered the **STRONG**! We were safe!

The ninja were tied up and taken away as Shrewdpaws squeaked angrily, "That parchment should have been mine! **Mine! Mine! Mine!**" Then he **stamped** his paws and began wailing like a spoiled mouselet.

Wild Willie snickered.

"Oh, stop your blubbering, Shrewdpaws.

Get them!

Get them!

Get them!

Did you really think you would get the parchment? It's a treasure from the past. That means it's not yours or mine. It belongs to **everyone**!"

Noblemouse nodded. "Very wise, Red Dragon. We will donate this parchment to the **Mouseum of Rodent History** in New Mouse City."

Wild Willie bowed. "So be it, Master," he said.

And so it was!

We returned to Mouse Island and **DONATED** the parchment to the Mouseum of Rodent History. Now it's there for everyone to enjoy. I give you my word, or my name isn't *Geronimo Stilton*!

WHAT TOOK YOU SO LONG?

After my trip, I took a few days off and then I went back to work at *The Rodent's Gazette*. My grandfather William Shortpaws, Thea, Benjamin, Trap, and all my coworkers were there to greet me. Word of our adventures in Japan had already reached New Mouse City.

"Hooray, Geronimo!"

"Welcome back!"

"Great job fighting those ninja!"

While everyone was cheering, Grandfather pulled me aside. "Okay, that's enough partying, Grandson. **NOW GET BACK TO WORK!** You've finally had a decent adventure and I want you to write about it **RIGHT N-O-W**! I want it done by early next week. Do you understand? *Get cracking!*"

What could I do? I locked myself in the office and began writing like a **mad mouse**. The following week I finished my new **BOOK**. Yep, that's right! It's the book you're reading now: *The Way of the Samurai*!

Thea was the first to read it. "Good for you, Geronimo!" she said when she was done. "I knew you needed a new **ADVENTURE**, and that the trip to **Japan** was perfect for you. I was right as usual! What else is new?!"

I sighed. My sister likes to take credit for **everything**.

For a while everything was back to **normal**. I went to work, came home, and relaxed with a book in my cozy mouse hole. Then one night, I decided to take a walk by the docks. Before long, I found myself in the little courtyard at **South Paw Square**. The garden looked the same, but there was a new outdoor restaurant. As I strolled closer, I noticed the rodents were eating raw clams. **CLAMS?** That got me thinking about Wild Willie's words:

"Stilton, you're as exciting as a raw clam!"

I grinned to myself. Well, that was before we went on our adventure to Japan. Now I knew I could be **strong** and **courageous**, just like a real samurai!

When I reached the karate dojo, I peered inside. I saw **CHOP CHOP** and **LOTUS SNOUt** training with my sister, **Thea**, and my friend **Bruce Hyena**! In the front of the room,

I even saw my little nephew **Benjamin** and his friend **BUGSY WUGSY** taking lessons with other young rodents!

I couldn't believe they were all learning karate!

As I watched, lots of students carrying sport bags pushed past me and headed into the **DOJO** for their own karate lessons.

For a minute I thought about my **comfy** pawchair at home. Then I looked at my family and friends inside the dojo. They were laughing and learning and getting stronger. Putting one paw before the other, I **followed** the students inside. Seeing me, Chop Chop, Lotus Snout, Hyena, Thea, Baby Bonsai, Benjamin, and Bugsy Wugsy ran to greet me.

"**Geronimo is here!**" they squeaked.

Then I saw Wild Willie in the corner.

"What took you so long, Stilton?" he said with a smile.

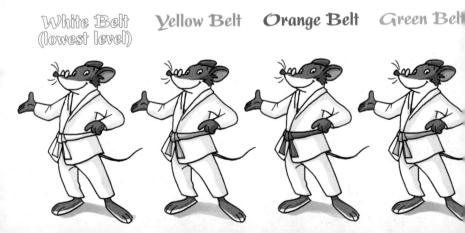

White Belt (lowest level)   Yellow Belt   Orange Belt   Green Belt

From that day on, things changed. Three times a week I took **KARATE LESSONS**, and eventually I even earned my black belt!

I'm now way more exciting than a raw clam!

Everyone was very proud of me. And after that, I went on to many more exciting **ADVENTURES** with Wild Willie. Was I scared? Of course! But I tried to remember what I had learned in Japan about courage and heart and the incredible **way of the samurai**!

Blue Belt   **Brown Belt**   **Black Belt (highest level)**

Don't miss any of my other fabumouse adventures!

#1 Lost Treasure of the Emerald Eye

#2 The Curse of the Cheese Pyramid

#3 Cat and Mouse in a Haunted House

#4 I'm Too Fond of My Fur!

#5 Four Mice Deep in the Jungle

#6 Paws Off, Cheddarface!

#7 Red Pizzas for a Blue Count

#8 Attack of the Bandit Cats

#9 A Fabumouse Vacation for Geronimo

#10 All Because of a Cup of Coffee

#11 It's Halloween, You 'Fraidy Mouse!

#12 Merry Christmas, Geronimo!

#13 The Phantom of the Subway

#14 The Temple of the Ruby of Fire

#15 The Mona Mousa Code

#16 A Cheese-Colored Camper

#17 Watch Your Whiskers, Stilton!

#18 Shipwreck on the Pirate Islands

#19 My Name Is Stilton, Geronimo Stilton

#20 Surf's Up, Geronimo!

#21 The Wild, Wild West

#22 The Secret of Cacklefur Castle

A Christmas Tale

#23 Valentine's Day Disaster

#24 Field Trip to Niagara Falls

#25 The Search for Sunken Treasure

#26 The Mummy with No Name

#27 The Christmas Toy Factory

#28 Wedding Crasher

#29 Down and Out Down Under

#30 The Mouse Island Marathon

#31 The Mysterious Cheese Thief

Christmas Catastrophe

#32 Valley of the Giant Skeletons

#33 Geronimo and the Gold Medal Mystery

#34 Geronimo Stilton, Secret Agent

#35 A Very Merry Christmas

#36 Geronimo's Valentine

#37 The Race Across America

#38 A Fabumouse School Adventure

#39 Singing Sensation

#40 The Karate Mouse

#41 Mighty Mount Kilimanjaro

#42 The Peculiar Pumpkin Thief

#43 I'm Not a Supermouse!

#44 The Giant Diamond Robbery

#45 Save the White Whale!

#46 The Haunted Castle

#47 Run for the Hills, Geronimo!

#48 The Mystery in Venice

#49 The Way of the Samurai

And coming soon!

#50 This Hotel Is Haunted!

THE KINGDOM OF FANTASY

THE QUEST FOR PARADISE:
THE RETURN TO THE KINGDOM OF FANTASY

THE AMAZING VOYAGE:
THE THIRD ADVENTURE IN THE KINGDOM OF FANTASY

Be sure to check out these exciting Thea Sisters adventures!

THEA STILTON AND THE DRAGON'S CODE

THEA STILTON AND THE MOUNTAIN OF FIRE

THEA STILTON AND THE GHOST OF THE SHIPWRECK

THEA STILTON AND THE SECRET CITY

THEA STILTON AND THE MYSTERY IN PARIS

THEA STILTON AND THE CHERRY BLOSSOM ADVENTURE

THEA STILTON AND THE STAR CASTAWAYS

THEA STILTON: BIG TROUBLE IN THE BIG APPLE

THEA STILTON AND THE ICE TREASURE

THEA STILTON AND THE SECRET OF THE OLD CASTLE

Meet
CREEPELLA VON CACKLEFUR

I, *Geronimo Stilton*, have a lot of mouse friends, but none as **spooky** as my friend CREEPELLA VON CACKLEFUR! She is an enchanting and MYSTERIOUS mouse with a pet bat named Bitewing. YIKES! I'm a real 'fraidy mouse, but even I think CREEPELLA and her family are AWFULLY fascinating. I can't wait for you to read all about CREEPELLA in these fa-mouse-ly funny and **spectacularly spooky** tales!

#1 THE THIRTEEN GHOSTS

#2 MEET ME IN HORRORWOOD

#3 GHOST PIRATE TREASURE

ABOUT THE AUTHOR

 Born in New Mouse City, Mouse Island, **GERONIMO STILTON** is Rattus Emeritus of Mousomorphic Literature and of Neo-Ratonic Comparative Philosophy. For the past twenty years, he has been running *The Rodent's Gazette*, New Mouse City's most widely read daily newspaper.

Stilton was awarded the Ratitzer Prize for his scoops on *The Curse of the Cheese Pyramid* and *The Search for Sunken Treasure*. He has also received the Andersen 2000 Prize for Personality of the Year. One of his bestsellers won the 2002 eBook Award for world's best ratlings' electronic book. His works have been published all over the globe.

In his spare time, Mr. Stilton collects antique cheese rinds and plays golf. But what he most enjoys is telling stories to his nephew Benjamin.

1. Main entrance
2. Printing presses (where the books and newspaper are printed)
3. Accounts department
4. Editorial room (where the editors, illustrators, and designers work)
5. Geronimo Stilton's office
6. Helicopter landing pad

THE RODENT'S GAZETTE

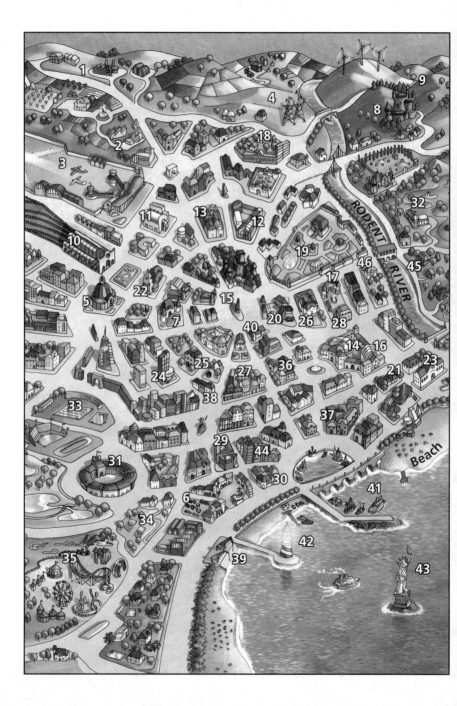

Map of New Mouse City

Brigand's Isle

This way to the Rodent Straits

Pirate Ship
of Cats

Tomcat Island

Cat's
Claw
Bay

Panther
Archipelago

Hamster Islands

Blue Dolphin
Bay

Swissville

Coral Reefs

This way
to the Mousific
Ocean

Stray
Cat
Harbor

Cheddarton

Mouseport

This way
to the
Ratlantic
Ocean

San Mouscisco

New Mouse City

Mousefort Beach

Furflung Island

This way to the Sea of Mice

N
W   E
S

MOUSE ISLAND

Map of Mouse Island

1. Big Ice Lake
2. Frozen Fur Peak
3. Slipperyslopes Glacier
4. Coldcreeps Peak
5. Ratzikistan
6. Transratania
7. Mount Vamp
8. Roastedrat Volcano
9. Brimstone Lake
10. Poopedcat Pass
11. Stinko Peak
12. Dark Forest
13. Vain Vampires Valley
14. Goose Bumps Gorge
15. The Shadow Line Pass
16. Penny Pincher Castle
17. Nature Reserve Park
18. Las Ratayas Marinas
19. Fossil Forest
20. Lake Lake
21. Lake Lakelake
22. Lake Lakelakelake
23. Cheddar Crag
24. Cannycat Castle
25. Valley of the Giant Sequoia
26. Cheddar Springs
27. Sulfurous Swamp
28. Old Reliable Geyser
29. Vole Vale
30. Ravingrat Ravine
31. Gnat Marshes
32. Munster Highlands
33. Mousehara Desert
34. Oasis of the Sweaty Camel
35. Cabbagehead Hill
36. Rattytrap Jungle
37. Rio Mosquito

Dear mouse friends,
Thanks for reading, and farewell
till the next book.
It'll be another whisker-licking-good
adventure, and that's a promise!

Geronimo Stilton